PIANO • VOCAL • GUITAR

MW00861860

CONTENTS

Hal Leonard Publishing Corporation
7777 West Bluemound Road P.O. Box 13819 Milwaukee, WI 53213

ROOM IN YOUR HEART

Words and Music by
PAUL WILLIAMS

SCROOGE

Words and Music by
PAUL WILLIAMS

14

gave a prize for be-ing mean, the win-ner would be him. Old
un-dis-put-ed mas-ter of the un-der-hand-ed deed. He

Scrooge, he loves __ his mon-ey 'cause he thinks __ it gives him pow-er. If
charg-es folks __ a for-tune for his dark __ and draft-y hous-es. Us

he be-came a fla-vor, you can bet he would be sour. __
poor folk live in mis-er-y. It's e-ven worse for mous-es.

(Spoken:) Please sir, I want some

ONE MORE SLEEP 'TIL CHRISTMAS

Words and Music by
PAUL WILLIAMS

D.S. al Coda

The

CODA

'Tis the sea-son to be jol-ly and joy - ous.

With a burst of plea-sure, we feel it ar - rive.

It's the sea - son when the Saints_ can em - ploy ___ us to

spread the news_ a-bout peace and to keep love a - live.

(Spoken:) Merry Christmas. So long. There's some-thin' in ___ the wind ___ to-day ___ that's

MARLEY AND MARLEY

Words and Music by
PAUL WILLIAMS

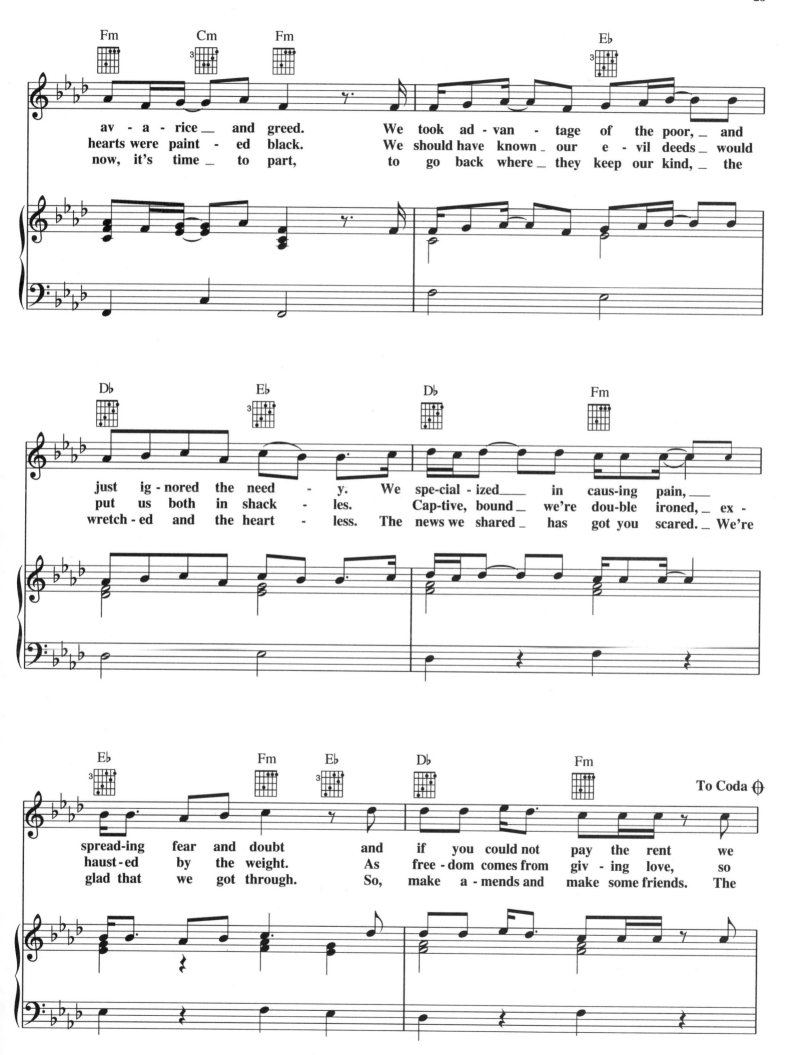

Doomed, Scrooge, _ you're doomed for all time. _ Your

fu - ture is a hor - ror sto - ry writ - ten by your crime. _ Your

chains are forged _ by what you say and do. _ So,

have your fun. When life is done a night - mare waits for you.

CHAIRMAN OF THE BOARD

Words and Music by
PAUL WILLIAMS

WHEN LOVE IS GONE

Words and Music by
PAUL WILLIAMS

IT FEELS LIKE CHRISTMAS

Words and Music by
PAUL WILLIAMS

42

heart, a spe-cial time of car - ing, the ways of love made clear. It is

the sea-son of the spir-it. The mes-sage, if we hear it, is make it last all

year.

It's in the sing-ing of the street cor-ner choir, it's go-ing home and get-ting

CHRISTMAS SCAT

Words and Music by
PAUL WILLIAMS

BLESS US ALL

Words and Music by
PAUL WILLIAMS

THANKFUL HEART

Words and Music by
PAUL WILLIAMS

With a

thank - ful heart, with an end - less joy, with a grow - ing fam- 'ly. Ev - 'ry
o - pen smile and with o - pen doors I will bid you wel - come. What is
thank - ful heart that is wide a - wake I do make this pro - mise: Ev - 'ry

girl and boy will be neph - ew and niece to me, (neph - ew and
mine is yours. With a glass raised to toast your health (with a glass raised to
breath I take will be used now to sing your praise (used now to

FINALE
WHEN LOVE IS FOUND/IT FEELS LIKE CHRISTMAS

Words and Music by
PAUL WILLIAMS

Lyrics:

Well, I met some-one who touched my soul and made my world brand new. There's part of me, a place in-side that now be-longs to you. The love we found, the love we

57